CHIPMUNK Alvin 987-4114   Timothy 271-3089
Carolyn 863-2382   DEER David 75
Chip 928-9023   Dominick 868-1422
Dale 627-   how 972-4419
Emily 825-1606
Hubert 652-7604
Simon 455-9001
Theodo   3-6767
OW B   4191
Elsie   976
Gr   90
H   2

Gulp!

R   0
Th   42
Zel   145
OYO   -0921
Esther 454-8279
Lawrence 771-1608
Vincent 779-5785
Wiley ....   rthur ... 690-1642
CROCODILE Gena   945-2338
Priscilla 576-0389
Stanley 485-2976
ROW Amanda 728-7846
Alex ....   e ... 567-3475
Bernard 531-6238
Darrell 924-1528
Frank 536-5612
Ruth 875-8043   EAGLE Lydia 372-1843

W9-BXJ-032

hone

by **Jamey Gambrell**

after *Telephone* by Kornei Chukovsky

Pictures by **Vladimir Radunsky**

N O R T H - S O U T H   B O O K S / N E W   Y O R K / L O N D O N

CAFE **Chez Porcupine**

Pachyderm Station

Jing-a-ling-a-ling.
The telephone
began to ring.
Elephant was on the line,
calling from Chez Porcupine.
"What do you want?"
I asked him up front.
"If I had my druthers,"
he said in a mutter,
"I'd order some more of your peanut butter."
"How much,
who's it for,
and what's the location?"
"Just a ton
for my son,
care of Pachyderm Station."

Then Crocodile called me in tears.
He was crying so loud
that I plugged up my ears.

"I need some galoshes
for me and my wife
and our cousin Natasha."

"Wait a minute!
Not so fast!
I sent you three pair
the week before last!"

"But that was back then.
We ate them all up.
We're hungry again.

"It's been ages since lunch
and we're dying to munch
more delicious,
nutritious
galoshes."

Then the doves
wanted gloves.

Then baboons asked for spoons.

Then Bear rang me up on the phone.
He grunted, he growled, and he groaned.

"Now, Bear, take it easy.
Don't moan and don't mumble.
I can't understand you at all
when you grumble."

But Bear could only cry
"BOO HOO!"
And why or how come,
I haven't a clue.

"Please hang up, Mr. Bear!"

Then the Stork called collect from the lake.
" I'm ill, send a pill,
I ate a whole snake
and my belly has started to ache."

Then Pig phoned to fret.
"I need a canary
To sing a duet."

"What?" I roared,
"You'd best see the vet!
Pigs dance jigs,
they don't sing duets.
No canary will sing with a hog.
Try the Frog."

Then Bear rang again:
"Help! Help! Poor Porpoise!
He swallowed a tortoise
and now he's in terrible pain."

This nonsense went on
all day long.
Jing-a-ling,
ting-a-ling,
ding-dong!

What a monumental bother!
First Ms. Seal called,
then Ms. Otter.

Last night I had a call from Kangaroo:
"Is this the home of Winnie-the-Pooh?"
I got so mad I stomped and pouted.
"No. NO!
This is MY house!" I shouted.
"Then where, I'd like to know, is Pooh?"
"I couldn't say.
Try

555-1212

I'm tired. I can't think.
I haven't slept a wink,
'Cause every time I blink—
jing-a-ling-a-ling-a-LING—
the telephone begins to ring!

"Who is it?"
"Rhinoceros."
"What's the trouble?"
"S.O.S.!
On the double!
Hippopotamus fell in the swamp!"

"In the swamp? Hippopotamus?
But it's bottomless!"

"He's up to his ears,
holding on to a log.
Hurry over right now,
or he'll drown in the bog!

"He'll die, he'll be lost to us—
our dear, dear Hippopotamus."

"O.K., O.K.,
I'm on my way."

Yuck. Just my luck,
to get stuck
hauling a hippo
out of the muck!

Jamey Gambrell is a critic and translator who has written extensively on contemporary American, European, and Russian art. She is a contributing editor at *Art in America,* and her articles on Russian culture and politics have appeared in the *Village Voice, Harper's,* and the *New York Review of Books.* She currently lives in Moscow. For children, she translated *The Story of a Boy Named Will, Who Went Sledding Down the Hill,* by Daniil Kharms.

Vladimir Radunsky, the son of a sailor, was born in the Ural Mountains of Russia. He has illustrated numerous books for children, including *The Maestro Plays, Hail to Mail, The Pup Grew Up!,* and *The Story of a Boy Named Will, Who Went Sledding Down the Hill,* which was published by North-South Books. He has won many awards—so many that we can't even count them.